The Apache
Indians

by Bill Lund

Content Consultant:
Dale Miles, San Carlos Apache Tribe
Historic Cultural Preservation Office

Bridgestone Books

an imprint of Capstone Press

Bridgestone Books are published by Capstone Press
818 North Willow Street, Mankato, Minnesota 56001
http://www.capstone-press.com

Library of Congress Cataloging-in-Publication Data
Lund, Bill, 1954-
    The Apache Indians/by Bill Lund.
       p. cm.--(Native peoples)
    Includes bibliographical references and index.
    Summary: Provides an overview of the past and present lives of the Apache people,
covering their daily life, customs, relations with the government and others, and more.
    ISBN 1-56065-561-5
    1. Apache Indians--History--Juvenile literature. 2. Apache Indians--Social life and
customs--Juvenile literature.
    [1. Apache Indians. 2. Indians of North America--New Mexico.] I. Title.
    II. Series: Lund, Bill, 1954-   Native peoples.

E99.A6L86 1998
973'.04972--dc21
                                                97-6396
                                                  CIP
                                                   AC

Photo credits
James C. Cokendolpher, 12
Chuck Place, cover, 6, 14
San Carlos Apache Tribe, 8, 10, 16
Unicorn/Richard Baker, 20
University of Oklahoma Libraries/Western History Collections, 18

Table of Contents

Map

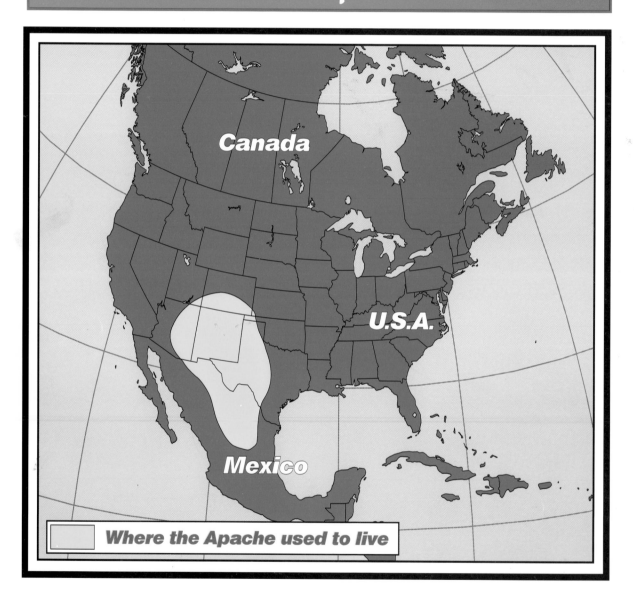

Canada

U.S.A.

Mexico

Where the Apache used to live

Fast Facts

Today, many Apache Indians live like most other North Americans. In the past, they practiced a different way of life. Their food, homes, and clothing helped make them special. These facts tell how the Apache once lived.

Food: The Apache ate deer, rabbits, and turkeys. They gathered fruits, nuts, plants, and honey.

Home: Most Apache lived in wickiups. A wickiup is a round house. It is covered with leaves and grass or animal skins. Some lived in tepees. A tepee is round with a pointed top. It is covered with animal skins.

Clothing: Apache women wore skirts and shirts made from animal skins. Men wore breechcloths in the summer. A breechcloth is a piece of deerskin. It passes between the legs and is tied with a belt. In the winter, men also wore shirts. Later, they used cloth to make clothes.

Language: The Apache language is part of the Athapaskan language family.

Past Location: The Apache's land covered an area from central Texas to central Arizona. It was also from southern Colorado to the Sierra Madre Mountains in Mexico.

Current Location: Today, they live in New Mexico, Oklahoma, and Arizona.

Special Events: Mountain Spirit Dances are important to the Apache. They believe Mountain Spirit Dances keep people from becoming ill. Puberty ceremonies honor young people who are becoming adults. A ceremony is an official practice.

The Apache People

The Apache have lived in North America for hundreds of years. The Apache were nomads. A nomad is a person who travels. Nomads do not stay in one place very long. The Apache traveled throughout the southwestern United States and northwestern Mexico.

Today, the Apache live on reservations. A reservation is land set aside for Native Americans. There are Eastern and Western Apache. The Eastern Apache reservations are in New Mexico and Oklahoma. The Western Apache reservations are in Arizona.

Today, the Apache live much like other North Americans. Many Apache work outdoors. Some Apache own cattle ranches. The Apache still remember their traditions. A tradition is a practice continued over many years.

The Apache still remember their traditions.

Homes, Food, and Clothing

Most Apache lived in round houses called wickiups. Women made a wickiup by bending young trees into a frame. They covered the frame with leaves, grasses, or animal skins.

Some Eastern Apache lived in tepees. A tepee has a round bottom and a pointed top. It is made from poles. The poles are covered with animal skins.

The men hunted food with bows and arrows. They hunted deer, rabbits, turkeys, and other animals. Women and children gathered fruits, nuts, and wild plants.

Apache women wore animal skin skirts and shirts. Men wore breechcloths. A breechcloth is a piece of deerskin. It passes between the legs and is tied with a belt. In winter men also wore shirts. Later, the Apache made clothing from cloth.

Apache women gathered wild plants for food.

Apache Baskets

The Apache are known for their baskets. In the past, they used baskets to gather and store food. They used other baskets to carry heavy loads. Today, many use baskets for decoration.

Apache women are skilled at making baskets. They make baskets from parts of plants. They use yucca, sumac, mulberry, and willow plants. Each type of plant is a different color. The colors make patterns in the baskets.

The Apache make special baskets called tus. Tus baskets are used to carry water. A tus basket starts out like a regular basket. Then the women cover the inside with pitch. Pitch is made from piñon pine. Pitch is thick like tar. The pitch makes the tus basket waterproof. Apache women still enjoy making all types of baskets. They sell many of their baskets.

The Apache carried water in tus baskets.

The Apache Family

In the past, the Apache lived in family groups. A family group included parents and their children. It could also include grandparents, aunts, and uncles.

Family groups lived together in one wickiup or tepee. Married couples lived with the wife's family. The couple's children became members of the mother's family.

A few family groups lived and traveled together. During the summer, they met with other Apache groups. These gatherings were important. Young men and women often found people to marry.

Today, Apache children go to school. They learn about Apache traditions. They also learn common subjects such as English, math, and science. Apache adults often work in areas near their reservation.

Western Apache families lived in wickiups.

Apache Religion

The Apache religion says there are many spirits. A religion is a set of beliefs that people follow. The Apache believe that everything in nature has a spirit. Spirits can be good or bad. Religion is part of the Apache's daily life.

There are many important religious ceremonies in Apache life. A ceremony is an official practice. Ceremonies are performed by a di-yin. A di-yin is a religious leader. Apache people sometimes dance in ceremonies. They wear beautiful traditional clothing. They ask for blessings when they dance.

Today, some Apache still practice their traditional religion. Others practice Christianity. Christianity is a religion based on the teachings of Christ.

Apache people sometimes dance in ceremonies.

Apache Government

Long ago, small groups of Apache families traveled together. Each group had its own leader. Sometimes they camped near other small groups. The small groups joined together are called a band. All of the Apache bands make up the Apache nation.

The Apache nation did not have a central government. Each band made its own treaties with the U.S. government. A treaty is an official agreement between governments.

The U.S. government did not understand the Apache system. It thought the treaties were with the entire Apache nation. This caused problems for the Apache and the United States.

Today, each Apache reservation has its own tribal government. A tribal council makes decisions for the reservation. The tribal council is lead by a chairperson.

Each Apache tribe has a tribal council chairperson.

Geronimo

Long ago, the Apache fought hard to keep their land and culture. A culture is the way of life of a group of people. The Mexicans tried to rule the Apache. Later, the U.S. government tried to take the Apache's land. The Apache fought them both.

Geronimo was born in 1829. His Apache name was Goyokla. It means One Who Yawns. The Mexicans gave him the name Geronimo. He was known as a fierce fighter. When the Mexicans saw him charging they yelled Geronimo. The Mexicans were praying for help in Spanish.

Geronimo was a respected war chief and holy man. He prayed to spirits for victory. But, many people feared Geronimo. For 10 years, he attacked villages. He and his band killed people. They stole supplies and horses.

In 1886, Geronimo turned himself over to U.S. troops. He lived the rest of his life in Fort Sill, Oklahoma. Fort Sill is a U.S. Army base.

Geronimo was a respected war chief and holy man.

Child of Water

The Apache told many stories called legends. Legends often explained things in nature. One legend tells how a young boy killed a monster.

Long ago, White Painted Woman lived on the earth. Four monsters also lived there. The monsters killed people. White Painted Woman gave birth to a son. His name was Child of Water.

One day, a monster tried to steal their food. Child of Water wanted to fight the monster. He and the monster agreed to a contest.

Both fighters had a chance to shoot four arrows. Child of Water picked up a blue rock. The rock was a good luck charm. The monster shot its arrows at Child of Water. None of the arrows hit him. Child of Water's fourth arrow hit the monster's heart.

As Child of Water grew, he killed the other three monsters. Ever since, the world has been safe for humans.

The Apache told many stories called legends.

Hands On: Hidden-Ball Game

The Apache often played the hidden-ball game. They played it around the fire at night. You can play a similar game.

What You Need

1 small rock	1 stick
1 blanket	8 small paper bags
4 or more players	

What You Do

1. Divide the players into two teams. There will be a hiding team and a guessing team.
2. The hiding team hides behind the blanket. They put the rock in one of the bags. Then they put the bags in a row. They take away the blanket.
3. The guessing team chooses one of its players. The chosen player is given a stick.
4. The hiding team makes noise to mix up the guesser.
5. The guesser tries to guess which bag holds the rock. The guesser uses the stick to point to that bag.
6. If the guesser is right, it becomes the guessing team's turn to hide the rock. They do not win any points. Only the hiding team can win points.
7. If the guesser is wrong, the hiding team wins 10 points. The hiding team hides the rock again.
8. The first team to score 100 points wins.

Words to Know

band (BAND)—many small family groups joined together

di-yin (DEE-in)—a religious leader

reservation (rez-ur-VAY-shuhn)—land set aside for Native Americans

tus (TUS)—a basket lined with piñon pitch and used to carry water

yucca (YUH-kuh)—a plant used for food and to make baskets

wickiup (WIK-ee-uhp)—a round house covered with leaves and grass or animal skins

Read More

Doherty, Craig A., and Katherine M. Doherty. *The Apaches and Navajos*. New York: Franklin Watts, 1989.

Fleischner, Jennifer. *The Apaches*. Brookfield, Conn.: The Millbrook Press, 1994.

Melody, Michael E. *The Apache*. New York: Chelsea House Publishers, 1989.

Useful Addresses

Apache
P.O. Box 1220
Anadarko, OK 73005

San Carlos Apache
P.O. Box 0
San Carlos, AZ 85550

Internet Sites

Geronimo: His Own Story
http://grid.let.rug.nl/~welling/usa/geronimo/
   geroni.htm

Native American Cultural Resources on the Internet
http://hanksville.phast.umass.edu/misc/
   NAresources.html

Index

DATE DUE
